Jackson & Auggie: Adventure in the Hudson Valley

A "Tail" by Two Sisters

Written by Renée Pearce

Illustrated by Kaylin Ruffino

Strategic Book Publishing and Rights Co.

Strategic Book Publishing and Rights Co.
12620 FM 1960, Suite A4-507
Houston, TX 77065
www.sbpra.com

ISBN: 978-1-60976-459-3

Dedicated to

Mom, Dad and Jay for your love and support

and to our pets for

giving us our inspiration

Renée and Kaylin Ages 5 & 2

Auggie and Jackson were cousins,
but best of friends they were too.

Jackson was a young Siamese cat, and Auggie,
a Boxer puppy through and through.

They had grown up together in a quaint little town,
located an hour past New York City.

They loved country life. They loved the lake region;
life was perfect for this doggie and kitty.

One summer day, they were looking for fun,
so off on a walk they went.

On and far they traveled,
walking and talking made them content.

When far from home they found themselves,
it was Jackson who realized they were lost.

But Auggie wanted to keep going,
so into the next town they crossed . . .

An unexpected adventure had begun;
excited and scared were the two.

Never had they been far from home,
but this was a chance to see something new!

The duo came upon a massive site. Located in
Washingtonville is a place called Brotherhood.

"It's the 'oldest winery in America,'" read Jack.
A historic place to explore, in all likelihood.

They joined the tour that had started
and learned all about the past.

They stomped some grapes and sipped some juice,
then left feeling silly, and sharing some laughs.

9

The journey continued west,
when they spotted the blackest dirt they had ever seen!

Auggie made a dash to dig,
while Jackson preferred to stay clean.

The dirt was soft and the farmland was rich,
when onions are what Auggie found—

Pine Island is known for their black dirt.
It is the finest for miles around!

As north the pair continued to move,
Jackson noticed something soaring high.

Flying saucers and UFOS
are common in Pine Bush skies.

Quickly they hurried past,
eager to see something new.

In Monroe they discovered cheese was created!
Velveeta, not anything bleu!

They also toured Museum Village,
a place that preserves the past.

They took a quick stop at the Gooseponds
and explored Airplane Park last.

The excitement was building with each stop made.
A true journey had begun—
what would their owners think of this escapade?

Auggie's stomach began to rumble,
but Jackson decided it was time to shop.

They headed toward Woodbury Common,
a number-one Hudson Valley hot spot!

Along the Hudson they roamed, 'til into Cornwall
where they heard—

Somewhere near laid Captain Kidd's treasure,
according to what historians say occurred!

Cornwall lies on the Hudson River,
which was cruised by many long ago.

Pirates' lost gold was the legend,
but where it's hidden no one knows.

Located in Newburgh, a little ways away,
is Washington's Headquarters,
where the first president and his wife had stayed!

Strategically located near West Point and with a great river view,
the president resided back in 1782.

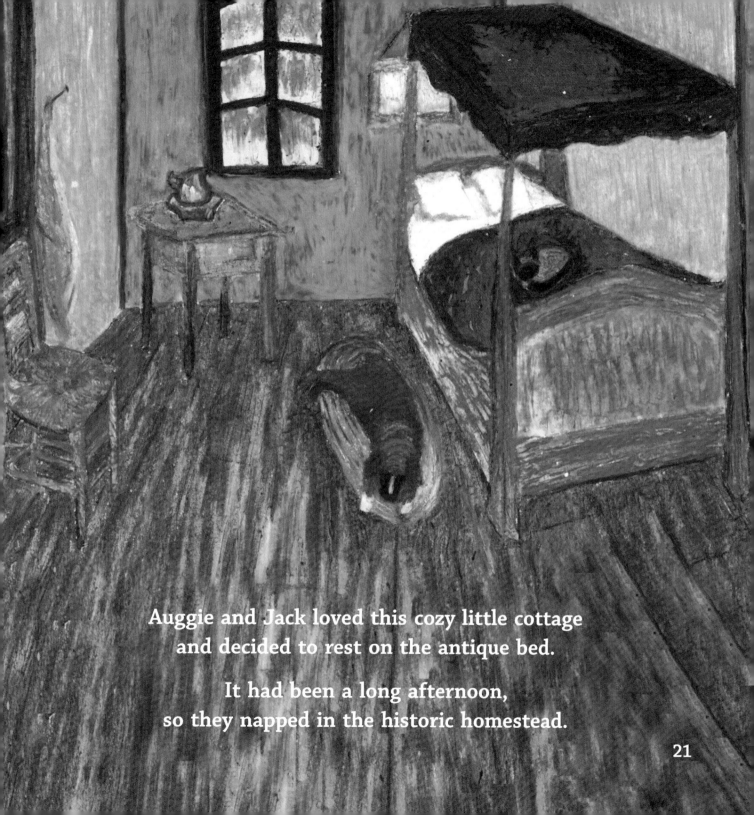

Auggie and Jack loved this cozy little cottage
and decided to rest on the antique bed.

It had been a long afternoon,
so they napped in the historic homestead.

21

How Auggie and Jack ended up
on a boat is still a mystery!

They sailed across the river
to the old artillery!

The castle was crumbling and
Bannerman's Island was spooky.

Still, the two friends move onward;
West Point was a great place to sightsee.

Auggie and Jackson were enchanted
from the museums to Michie Stadium.

The military academy and its soldiers
are surely second to none!

The last place that the pals wanted to
discover and explore

was Bear Mountain State Park.
It is a zoo, campground, and more!

They roamed around the park 'til
they found the infamous carousel.

Round and round they rode 'til
it was time to say farewell.

After a momentous day, it was time to go home.
They missed their families and Auggie wanted a bone!

Paw-in-paw, they began the trip back.
Until the next time, Jack was so tired he needed a piggyback!

© Salvador Dalí, Fundació Gala-Salvador Dalí / Artists Rights Society (ARS), New York 2011

Grant Wood, Young Corn, 1931. Oil on Masonite panel, 24 x 29 7/8 in. Collection of the Cedar Rapids Community School District, on loan to the Cedar Rapids Museum of Art.

© Salvador Dalí, Fundació Gala-Salvador Dalí / Artists Rights Society (ARS), New York 2011

Lascaux, Primier taureau. N. Aujoulat © Ministére de la Culture et de la Communication, France/ Centre National de Préhistoire.

© 2011 The Andy Warhol Foundation for the Visual Arts, Inc. / Artists Rights Society (ARS), New York

POINTILLISM
Late 1880's
Pages 8-9

Branching from Impressionism, Georges Seurat developed this technique in 1886. *Pointillism* is a method where small dots of pure color form an image among their mix.

AMERICAN FOLK ART
Eighteenth and Nineteenth Century
Pages 10-11

Specific to a particular culture, is *American Folk Art*.
Grant Wood is famous for his paintings, used as decoration for the most part.

SURREALISM
1920's
Pages 12-13

Salvador Dali was a surrealist; bizarre and weird images is what he is famous for. This illustration was based on *Les Elephantes*. All artwork in this movement has a surprise in store.

CAVE PAINTINGS
Neolithic Period: c. 9500 BC
Pages 14-15

Most famously found in Lascaux, France, so to speak, a prehistoric form of communication, *Cave Paintings* are unique.

POP ART
1960's
Pages 16-17

Andy Warhol, known for his repetitive images, was a leading figure in the movement known as *pop art*.
A painter, printmaker and filmmaker, yet commercial advertising is where he got his start.

Fluke Fishing 2008
Kaylin Ruffino

ABORIGINAL ART
Pages 18-19

Australian cultures pass down stories called "dreamtime" from one generation to the next, through paintings made of dots, traditional earth tone colors work best.

Bedroom in Arles 1888
Vincent Van Gogh

IMPRESSIONISM
Nineteenth Century
Pages 20-21

Mostly done with landscapes, *Impressionism* is the style of artist Vincent Van Gogh. This illustration is based on *Bedroom in Arles*, as some of you may know.

National Archives Photo No. 79-AA-S02 (Ansel Adams Series, 1941).

MONOCHROME PHOTOGRAPHY
Pages 22-23

Ansel Adams was an artist best known for his photographs in black and white, as was Alfred Stieglitz- whose modern art photos used shades of dark and light.

Den Haag, Koninklijke Bibliotheek + shelf mark.

MEDIEVAL ART
The Middle Ages
Pages 24-25

In the Western world, over a vast scope of time and place for more than a thousand years-
From Heraldry to Illuminated manuscripts, tapestries, and mosaics, artists taught a message for all to hear.

FRENCH POST-IMPRESSIONISM
1880–1920
Pages 26-27

Henri Rousseau's paintings are scenes that are primitive native.
Having never seen the jungle, this artist was very creative!

Exotic Landscape with Playing Monkeys 1910 Henri Rousseau

About the Author and Illustrator

Renée & Auggie
2011

Renée Pearce and Kaylin Ruffino are sisters who grew up in Monroe, New York. Renée currently resides in Highland Mills, NY, and Kaylin in Pine Bush, NY. Renée is a middle school teacher for gifted and talented students and Kaylin teaches middle school art.

Kaylin & Jackson
2011

Renée and Kaylin wrote *Jackson and Auggie: Adventure in the Hudson Valley* to be used as a teaching tool in addition to entertainment. They are both inspired by their parents and families, and the beautiful region of the country where they live.